To Tyler
and
Reese.
Love.
Mimi T Popple

The Night
Before Christmas

We dedicate this book to all of the artists who have created beautiful pictures for children's books, especially the Anonymous and the Unknown who labored endlessly, fruitfully, and with little recognition.
— H. D. and C. E.

This edition published in 2005 by Chronicle Books LLC.

This edition retains the spelling and grammar of the original 1823 edition.

Copyright © 1998 by Blue Lantern Studio.
All rights reserved.

Book design by Juliana Van Horn.
Manufactured in China.
ISBN 0-8118-5028-5

The Library of Congress has cataloged the previous edition as follows:
Moore, Clement Clarke, 1779-1863
The night before Christmas : a classic illustration edition:
selected illustrations from over 20 classic editions / by Clement Moore;
compiled and arranged by Cooper Edens and Harold Darling.
cm.
Summary: The well-known poem about a famous Christmas visitor is accompanied by illustra-
tions by various nineteenth and twentieth-century artists.
ISBN 0-8118-1712-1
1. Santa Claus—Juvenile poetry. 2. Christmas—Juvenile poetry. 3. Children's poetry, American.
[1. Christmas—Poetry. 2. Santa Clause—Poetry. 3. American poetry. 4. Narrative poetry.]
I. Edens, Cooper. II. Darling, Harold. III. Title.
PS2429.M5N5   1997c
811'.2—dc21   97-4101
CIP
AC

Distributed in Canada by Raincoast Books
9050 Shaughnessy Street, Vancouver, British Columbia V6P 6E5

10 9 8 7 6 5 4 3 2 1

Chronicle Books LLC
85 Second Street, San Francisco, California 94105

www.chroniclekids.com

The Night Before Christmas

by
Clement C. Moore

A CLASSIC ILLUSTRATED EDITION

Compiled by Cooper Edens and
Harold Darling

chronicle books · san francisco

∾ PREFACE ∾

Clement Moore's imagination has defined the way we celebrate Christmas. In his 1822 poem *A Visit From St. Nicholas,* now known as *The Night Before Christmas,* Moore visualized Santa's Christmas Eve activities so vividly that we have since seen the season through his eyes. For the first time, Santa Claus traveled in a flying sleigh drawn by reindeer and slid down the chimney with a sack full of toys. These images have become Christmas legend. And generations of children have been enchanted by the thought of catching a glimpse of this mythical man in the middle of the night.

This edition of *The Night Before Christmas* is unique. The original poem is illustrated by some of the most renowned book illustrators of the last century. Chosen from our collection of antique picture books are the images we believe best bring each stanza to life. From Arthur Rackham to Jessie Willcox Smith to W. W. Denslow, over twenty distinct visions of the night before Christmas come together here to tell one glorious story.

Because each illustrator had a different vision, you will see many different Santas. Some are wise and stoic, some small and elfish, some tall and majestic, some jolly, some zany, some fierce, some saintly. What we learn is that Santa Claus is not just one figure, but many. In our imaginations he has grown and become more universal than any single portrait.

We feel enriched by the time we have spent with Clement Moore's classic poem. We hope you will enjoy it as much as we have.

— *Cooper Edens & Harold Darling*

T was the night before Christmas,
When all through the house
Not a creature was stirring,
    not even a mouse;

he stockings were hung by the chimney with care,
In hopes that St. Nicholas soon would be there.
The children were nestled all snug in their beds,
While visions of sugar-plums danced through their heads;

nd mamma in her kerchief, and I in my cap,
Had just settled our brains for a long winter's nap,
When out on the lawn there arose such a clatter,
I sprang from my bed to see what was the matter.

way to the window I flew like a flash,
Tore open the shutters and threw up the sash.

he moon on the breast of the new-fallen snow
Gave the lustre of mid-day to objects below;
When, what to my wondering eyes should appear,
But a miniature sleigh and eight tiny reindeer,

ith a little old driver, so lively and quick,
I knew in a moment it must be St. Nick.
More rapid than eagles his coursers they came,
And he whistled, and shouted, and called them by name:

ow Dasher! now, Dancer! now, Prancer! and Vixen!
On, Comet! on, Cupid! on, Donder and Blitzen!
To the top of the porch! to the top of the wall!
Now dash away! dash away! dash away all!"

s dry leaves that before the wild hurricane fly,
When they meet with an obstacle, mount to the sky,
So up the house-top the coursers they flew,
With the sleighful of toys, and St. Nicholas too.

nd then in a twinkling, I heard on the roof
The prancing and pawing of each little hoof.
As I drew in my head, and was turning around,
Down the chimney St. Nicholas came with a bound.

He was dressed all in fur from his head to his foot.
And his clothes were all tarnished with ashes and soot:
A bundle of toys he had flung on his back,
And he looked like a peddlar just opening his pack.

His eyes, how they twinkled! his dimples, how merry!
His cheeks were like roses, his nose like a cherry!
His droll little mouth was drawn up like a bow,
And the beard on his chin was as white as the snow;

The stump of a pipe he held tight in his teeth,
And the smoke, it encircled his head like a wreath.
He had a broad face, and a little round belly
That shook, when he laughed, like a bowl full of jelly.

e was chubby and plump—a right jolly old elf—
And I laughed, when I saw him, in spite of myself;
A wink of his eye, and a twist of his head,
Soon gave me to know I had nothing to dread.

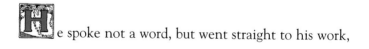

He spoke not a word, but went straight to his work,

nd filled all the stockings; then turned with a jerk,

nd laying his finger aside of his nose,
And giving a nod, up the chimney he rose.

He sprang to his sleigh, to the team gave a whistle,
And away they all flew, like the down of a thistle,

But I heard him exclaim, e're he drove out of sight,
"Happy Christmas to all, and to all a good-night!"

Front Cover: Unknown. postcard, circa 1908. ❧ *Casewrap:* Jessie Willcox Smith. *Twas the Night Before Christmas,* 1912. ❧ *Back Cover:* Margaret Evans Price. *The Night Before Christmas,* 1917. ❧ *Half-title:* Unknown. postcard, circa 1907. ❧ *Copyright Page:* Elizabeth MacKinstry. *The Night Before Christmas,* 1928. ❧ *Title Page:* Unknown. *St. Nicholas* magazine, circa 1900. ❧ *Opposite Preface:* Unknown. *The Night Before Christmas,* n.d. ❧ *Preface:* Thomas Nast. *Thomas Nast Christmas Drawings,* 1890. ❧ *Initial Cap Letters:* Jessie Willcox Smith. *Twas the Night Before Christmas,* 1912. ❧ *Page 10:* Unknown. *The Night Before Christmas,* n.d. ❧ *11:* Jessie Willcox Smith. *Twas the Night Before Christmas,* 1912. ❧ *12:* Arthur Rackham. *The Night Before Christmas,* 1931. ❧ *13:* Unknown. *Visit from St. Nicholas,* 1890. ❧ *14:* W. W. Denslow. *Denslow's Night Before Christmas,* 1902. ❧ *15:* Jessie Willcox Smith. *Twas the Night Before Christmas,* 1912. ❧ *16:* W. W. Denslow. *Denslow's Night Before Christmas,* 1902. ❧ *17:* Unknown. *Visit from St. Nicholas,* 1890. ❧ *18:* Joseph Cummings Chase. *The Night Before Christmas,* 1899. ❧ *19:* Unknown. *The Night Before Christmas, or A Visit of St. Nicholas,* 1896. ❧ *20-21:* Unknown. *Visit from St. Nicholas,* 1890. ❧ *22:* W. W. Denslow. *Denslow's Night Before Christmas,* 1902. ❧ *23:* Arthur Rackham. *The Night Before Christmas,* 1931. ❧ *24:* Unknown. *The Night Before Christmas, or A Visit of St. Nicholas,* 1896. ❧ *25:* Unknown. *Visit from St. Nicholas,* 1890. ❧ *26:* A.E.K. *The Night Before Christmas,* 1918. ❧ *27:* Unknown. postcard, circa 1900. ❧ *28:* Jessie Willcox Smith. *Twas the Night Before Christmas,* 1912. ❧ *29:* Unknown. *The Night Before Christmas, or A Visit of St. Nicholas,* 1896. ❧ *30:* Unknown. *The Night Before Christmas,* n.d. ❧ *31:* Jessie Willcox Smith. *Twas the Night Before Christmas,* 1912. ❧ *32:* E. Boyd Smith. *Santa Claus and All About Him,* 1908. ❧ *33:* B. Geyser. *The Night Before Christmas,* 1885. ❧ *34-35:* Unknown. *Visit from St. Nicholas,* 1890. ❧ *36:* A.E.K. *The Night Before Christmas,* 1918 ❧ *37:* Joseph Cummings Chase. *The Night Before Christmas,* 1899. ❧ *38-39:* Unknown. *The Night Before Christmas, or A Visit of St. Nicholas,* 1896. ❧ *40:* Unknown. *The Night Before Christmas,* n.d. ❧
List of Illustrators: Elizabeth MacKinstry.
The Night Before Christmas, 1928.